Frank Taylor

Regent Moray

Frank Taylor

Regent Moray

ISBN/EAN: 9783337278328

Printed in Europe, USA, Canada, Australia, Japan

Cover: Foto ©Raphael Reischuk / pixelio.de

More available books at **www.hansebooks.com**

The Regent Moray

THE

STANHOPE ESSAY

1895

BY

FRANK TAYLOR

SCHOLAR OF LINCOLN COLLEGE

'Qui didicit, patriae quid debeat et quid amicis'

Oxford

B. H. BLACKWELL, 50 & 51, BROAD STREET

London

SIMPKIN, MARSHALL, HAMILTON KENT & CO.

—

MDCCCXCV

DOUBTLESS some apology is due for the presumption of attempting to write anything fresh about Mary Stuart. But if it be fresh, at least it is not scandalous.

I do not find Moray a saint or Mary an angel. The simple method, which so many historians have favoured, of exalting the one by depressing the other, was never to my thinking justified by the existing evidence. I have aimed at reconciling these orthodox antagonisms. But the limits of time and space have allowed me merely to suggest the lines upon which such a reconciliation might conceivably be effected.

THE REGENT MORAY.

THE origin of the singular interest which attaches to the
history of the Sixteenth Century is not far to seek. It was
the period of transition, through which mediæval Europe
passed and from which modern Europe emerged. It was a
century of revolution, distinguished by a universality and
a complexity of change that are alike unexampled. A fresh
impulse was imparted to almost every department of thought
or action. The Reformation of the Christian Church, the
Renaissance in literature and the fine arts, the practice of
the new diplomacy by such consummate masters as Machiavelli, Cromwell, and the Guises, the discovery and develop-
ment of the New World, which had made Spain the
wealthiest power on the continent, the success of the new
tactics, whereby Swiss and Spanish infantry had been trained
to face the feudal cavalry of France, all these combined to
effect a transformation absolutely without parallel in the
history of the human race.

No aspect of this many-sided movement is more conspicuous than the growth—it might almost be called the
birth—of international politics. Thanks to the wisdom of
Ferdinand and the inexhaustible riches of the West, Spain
held the foremost position in Europe. France was her
closest competitor, for France, through the sagacious policy
of Louis the Eleventh, was at length sufficiently united to
assume that place, which, by her natural resources and the
number and military genius of her people, she had always
been qualified to occupy. England, it was painfully obvious
to her wisest statesmen, was only a second-rate power. She
had not stood still. She had progressed, slowly indeed, but
on lines which, as subsequent events have shown, were safer
and more enduring than those of her precocious rivals. But
temporarily she was eclipsed. Englishmen, whose diplomatic
horizon had always been bounded by the killing of Frenchmen, were now confronted with a very different France to
that which the accident of feudal disorganisation had so often
exposed to their mercy. The day was long gone by when a
single Agincourt could make a population of some four
millions master of another, at least three times that number.
A country, the insular situation of which was her chief, if not
her only, defence from the fate of the Netherlands, must be

content to pocket her pride and watch her opportunity. In the meantime her greatest victories were to be won in the politician's cabinet, a fact which Henry the Seventh was quick to recognise. His policy of peace, humiliating as it might appear to those that inherited the traditions of Edward the Third and Henry the Fifth, laid the foundations of England's ultimate greatness. Henry the Eighth, by the most dexterous manipulation, contrived to cut a showy figure among the princes of the continent. Both father and son succeeded in concealing their weakness while they gained that time, which was the one thing most needful to their schemes for minimising it.

Prominent among these was the Union with Scotland. Both peoples had everything to gain from such a consummation. If England was only a second-rate power in Europe, Scotland, except as a vantage ground to annoy her from, was altogether insignificant. By a union of the two Crowns the lesser country would be raised to a position of honourable equality with the greater, and the greater, while she received a valuable acquisition of fighting strength, would be rid for ever of a permanent source of anxiety and loss. Certainly for England the conversion of her old enemy into a new friend was doubly to be desired. Scotland, in the language of parliamentary parties, would "count two upon a division."

The plain duty of a Scottish statesman was to utilise that importance, which by force of circumstances his country had acquired, in procuring such a form of Union as was most gratifying to the patriotism of a proud, sensitive people. He must not allow himself to be bullied into giving "gold for bronze," nor must he temporise till England was strong enough to demand where she was now compelled to treat. He must watch for the accepted time, and then act without fear and without hesitation. Meanwhile he might find work enough and to spare in educating his countrymen to see that autonomy was the merest sentiment, when autonomy meant only contempt abroad and the chronic devastation of the borders at home.

For the obstacles were neither few nor small. There was the racial antipathy, renewed again and again on many a sanguinary battlefield since Northallerton, and perpetually smouldering along the banks of the Tweed. There was that sensitiveness of the Scottish people, peculiar to nationalities as to individuals, who are for ever imagining some affront to their poverty or their insignificance. There was the arrogance of the English sovereigns, who claimed, and had more than once attempted to enforce, a feudal authority over the sister kingdom. Finally, there was the ancient alliance with France, with nearly two centuries of familiar ties and old associations clustering about it. Scotchmen had fought side by side with Frenchmen in the Hundred Years War. The cadets of noble houses in Picardy or Touraine had been sent over seas to win their spurs in "the Debatable Land" with the Armstrongs and the Hepburns. For generations Scottish gentlemen and younger sons had formed the bodyguard of the kings of France.

And then, as though the matter were not already hard enough to tax to the uttermost the ingenuity of diplomats in an age of diplomacy, there came the Reformation to complicate it. Henry the Eighth's quarrel with the Pope was one more drop in the cup of "southron iniquity." At Pinkie the pikemen, who ten years later were wrecking monasteries and mobbing priests, taunted the retreating English cavalry as "heretic dogs."

But the Reformation carried with it its own remedy, the certain, if tardy, growth of a Protestant party in Scotland. The main obstacles to the Union were those already enumerated, the character of Henry the Eighth on the one hand, and of the Scottish people on the other. The former more than neutralised the good effects that might have sprung from the marriage of a daughter of England with James the Fourth; the latter had never conceived of the Union, or conceived of it only as the "southron's" name for servitude. The nation as a whole did not love the French, for it was not in their character to love any foreigner. But as long as the designs of the House of Guise upon their independence were unhatched, or at least undeveloped, they valued that alliance, which was valued in return. When in 1537 Magdalen de Valois became the wife of James the Fifth, and, still more, when in the following year her place was taken, at her untimely death, by Mary of Guise, the prospects of the Union seemed as remote as ever they had seemed in all the years that followed Flodden. The King, bent on asserting a prerogative, which had grown weak for want of exercise, called in the Church to his assistance in the struggle with the more refractory of the nobles. And the Church, fearful of the infection of that policy of Henry's in matters ecclesiastical, which had already become the scandal of Christendom, was all for the ancient league with France. But the coalition, while it broke the power of the Douglases, drove them and others like them into Henry's arms. Then was formed the nucleus of that company of political hucksters, "the assured lords" as they were euphemistically termed, who were to do the dirty work of the English Government in Scotland for the next sixty years.

In December, 1542, when the news of the fiasco of Solway Moss was brought to the dying King, and when the prospects of an honourable Union between the nations seemed at their darkest, a boy was studying at the University of St. Andrew's who was destined to have a larger hand than any living man in the conciliation of the ancient foes. Among the many virtues of James the Fifth continence found no place. He inherited to the full the voluptuous temper of a mother, who was the sister of Henry the Eighth, and of a father, who had preferred the caresses of Lady Heron to his own life and the lives of his subjects. James Stuart, the offspring of his amour with that Margaret Erskine, who afterwards became the wife of the Douglas of Lochleven, was born in 1531. A legend declares that the lady was carried off upon her wedding-day and privately married to the youthful king. However that may be, the child was regarded as a bastard, and was brought up in the company of three of his bastard brothers at St. Andrew's, of which he was made Commendator at the age of seven. He was a student in the University of that town when his father died, though no record remains of his having graduated there, and he appears to have resided occasionally under the care of his mother at Lochleven. In 1548 he accompanied his sister on her adventurous voyage to France, but his sojourn in Paris was brief, too brief for him to have imbibed much store of learning at those famous " scolis," which he and his brothers are said to have attended. Before the year was out he was back in Scotland, where his talent for action found occasion to display itself. With a raw levy of the district he confronted an English force, which had suddenly descended on the coast of Fife. The undisciplined militia, terrified by the artillery of the invaders, were fast falling into confusion, when the youthful Commendator (he was only seventeen), encouraging them by word and example, led on a second charge, which drove the English to their ships. Thus early did he furnish a proof of that vigour of character which history has more than once remarked in the children of illicit love.

In civil affairs, the Lord James, though he had not as yet achieved renown, so acquitted himself as to earn the respect of all. He was present at that ecclesiastical council of 1549, when Scottish Churchmen, fearful of the times, essayed to set their house in order. In 1550 he visited France in the train of Mary of Guise, to whose interest he had not unnaturally attached himself, and in the ensuing year he obtained his legitimation. When the Estates met in 1554 to ratify Mary's regency, the most active and influential of her supporters was the Commendator of St. Andrew's.

Already the Reformation had secured some foothold in Scotland. All parties were agreed in reprehending the internal abuses of the Church, but doctrinal heretics were exposed to stern repression. Persecution, however was on a small scale, probably by reason of the paucity of convinced

Protestants. The real danger lay in the avarice of the nobility and gentry, who, where the pocket was concerned, could be infected by the example even of an English king. All the conditions which preceded Cromwell's dissolution of the monasteries, were reproduced in a more aggravated form. Great as had been the riches of the Church of England, in Scotland, as compared with the total wealth of the nation, they were far greater. Horrible as had been the revelations of English monastic life, the open, flaunting, licentiousness of Scottish clerics seemed to point to a yet more horrible, secret corruption. It was a poorer and a hungrier laity than that of England, and it had a richer spoil to seize, and a fairer plea for seizing it.

The necessary impetus came from those genuine reformers whose numbers had grown with the growing distaste for burning, and with the preaching and teaching of English refugees from the persecution of Mary Tudor. In 1557 the principal upholders of Protestant doctrine subscribed a "band," as was the national custom of those who were pledged to some important enterprise, whereby they bound themselves to advance, to the utmost of their united powers, the work of the Reformation in Scotland. The Lord James, now in his twenty-sixth year, and high in favour and confidence with the Queen-Regent, was the most prominent among the Lords of the Congregation, as the leaders of the movement were termed. Mary appears to have regarded their doings with indifference, if not with actual favour. The Protestant party had supported her in her struggle with the Hamiltons, and continued to support her in her policy of a French marriage for her daughter. In the winter of this same year, 1557, she despatched the Lord James with other ambassadors to arrange the match.

That hatred of England, which had risen to such a pitch after the battle of Pinkie that English prisoners were purchased for slaughter from the French auxiliaries, still animated the great mass of the nation. Nor was there any likelihood of improvement, as long as the furious policy, which Henry had inaugurated, found favour with his successors. When the Lord James passed over to France to arrange his sister's marriage, it seemed as though no power on earth could bring about a reconciliation. But the House of Guise were fated to effect the very consummation which they most detested. The specious demand, made in the Dauphin's name for the Crown Matrimonial of Scotland, first opened the Commendator's eyes to the projects of that ambitious family. If he had, as yet, but an imperfect insight into their larger schemes, he could at least see through their transparent design for converting his country into an appanage of theirs. How far the darkest suspicions were

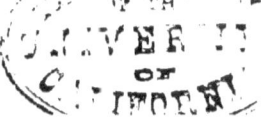

aroused, is attested by the current belief that poison was secretly administered to the ambassadors of Scotland. It is certain that three of them died in France, possibly of the plague. What militates against the truth of the story is the sheer stupidity of such a deed, not its atrocity, which, where the Guises are concerned, tends rather to its confirmation.

The Lord James was speedily required to act upon the judgment he had formed. Early in 1559 the Queen-Regent received certain instructions from her brothers, which, however much they might offend against her better judgment, she had no choice but to obey. It fell to her share, reluctant agent as she was, to work out an essential detail of that gigantic conspiracy which was already threatening the Reformation. A new Queen sat on the English throne, whose policy, though but a half-hearted Protestant herself, was to pose as the champion of Protestantism. Her destruction had been at once determined, but obviously it must come from that most vulnerable quarter, the northern frontier. It was for the Queen-Regent to begin the work by rooting out the heresy which she had allowed to attain to such proportions. The Protestants of Scotland would hardly tolerate an attack upon their English brethren. As they had now become too powerful to be disregarded, they must be destroyed.

It is unnecessary to dwell at length upon the miserable struggle that ensued. The preachers were summoned to Stirling to answer for their conduct, but at Perth so numerous and influential a company attended them that, on condition of its dispersal, the Regent promised to withdraw the citations. She broke her promise, and Knox and his brethren were outlawed. Then came those scenes of organised violence, which have branded the Reformation for all time with the reproach of vandalism. Lawless mobs, intoxicated with the rhetoric of the pulpit, made such havoc of monasteries and churches as filled all men of moderation and decent culture with intense disgust. The Regent moved on Perth, but her little force of disciplined Frenchmen was unequal to the assault. The Lord James and Argyle, who had married his sister, the Lady Jane, still lingered at her side in hope of effecting some accommodation. They succeeded in arranging terms, which were no sooner signed than broken. For the second time the Regent made it clear that, in pursuing her brothers' ends, she was bent on adopting their familiar methods of duplicity. Argyle and the Lord James, whose honours were concerned in the preservation of the treaty, went over to the Congregation, leaving the Regent almost alone with her Frenchmen. The patriotic side of the quarrel was now uppermost. The national liberty was imperilled by a coalition of France, Spain, and the Papacy.

When the armies faced each other on Coupar Moor it was as much the unsteadiness of his Scotch auxiliaries as the strength of the enemy's position which induced D'Oyselles to decline the combat.

The Lord James was already the most important personage in Scotland. The Regent used every endeavour to detach him from the Congregation. Foiled in this, she diligently propagated the slander that he was aiming at his sister's crown. The King of France was informed that "a bastard son to James the Fifth, called Prior de St. Andre, intended under cover of religion to usurp the kingdom to himself." It was one of those lies which admit only of denial and not of refutation. Suspicion was excited, more than one adherent of the Congregation began to falter, and the recent proceedings of the Lords incurred all the odium which attaches to sedition.

Reinforced from France and strongly entrenched at Leith the Regent bade defiance to her dispirited enemies. Henry the Second was dead, and though the boy, who was husband to the Queen of Scots, reigned in his stead, the Guises governed absolutely. The arms of Scotland and England were quartered with those of France, and every preparation made to uphold the claim thus arrogantly advertised. The time had come for Elizabeth to interfere. The imminence of the danger got the better of her disinclination to assist rebellious subjects. Moreover it was not, she pretended, as their ally, but as the feudal suzerain of their absent Queen that she was sending her armies to the siege of Leith. The negotiations were difficult and protracted. That they reached a successful issue was largely owing to the exertions of William Maitland of Lethington, the Regent's Secretary, a patriotic statesman, whose plain speaking in the fortress at Leith had rendered his continuance there impossible.

The armies of the two nations side by side—an unwonted spectacle—pushed on the siege with vigour. In June, 1560, the Regent died, worn out with anxiety and grief. Her death aroused the sympathy of all. Universally recognised to be the victim of a policy she detested, she never entirely lost that love and respect which her frank, generous, nature had secured her among a people notoriously suspicious of the foreigner. The Lord James, who had served her faithfully and well till personal loyalty conflicted with a larger duty, stood weeping at her bedside. To him she committed the safety of his sister and his country, and with words of penitence and warning on her lips "ended her life most Christianly."

She was avenged upon her family by the total miscarriage of that enterprise, to which she had been sacrificed. In July the garrison of Leith surrendered upon conditions, which afterwards became famous under the name of the Treaty of Edinburgh. In August the Estates met, passed the treaty, disestablished the Church, and set up in its place that form of Protestantism which is identified with the names of Calvin and of Knox. Sir James Sandilands, a knight of Rhodes, was dispatched to France to obtain the Queen's signature to these acts, but by the contrivance of the Guises both he and his mission were treated with contumely. But the death in a few months of Francis the Second changed the whole aspect of affairs. Catherine de Medici, the implacable enemy of the young widow, became Queen-Regent of France, and the Guises had enough to do to secure their own safety.

Mary was now at liberty to return to Scotland. She had nothing to detain her in France, on the contrary, she had one of the best reasons a woman can have for quitting it. As soon as her intentions were known she was visited by her brother, who assured her of the loyalty of her countrymen and placed his own services entirely at her disposal. She was visited also by Leslie, Bishop of Ross, who represented the party of the old Church in general and the Earl of Huntly in particular. His instructions were to promise her an army of twenty thousand men, provided she would land at Aberdeen and place herself at their head. Before deciding she prudently consulted her uncles and the gentlemen who had served her mother in Scotland. The general opinion was for her " to accommodate herself discreetly and gently to her own subjects, to be most familiar with my Lord James, . . . and with the Earl of Argyle, . . . and to use the Secretary Lidington and the Laird of Grange most tenderly in all their affairs." And surely such advice must have coincided with the inclinations of a girl of nineteen, who possessed no first-hand acquaintance with politics and no real experience of her countrymen. If she returned at all, she would naturally prefer to return as an angel of peace, not as a ringleader of warring factions. Huntly's offer was gracefully declined, and the Lord James hastened home to prepare for her arrival. Not without misgiving, Mary made ready to follow him. At the best it was something of a leap in the dark, as may be gathered from an examination of the factors which composed the political situation in her native land.

English historians have found a broad division of Scottish parties into Francophiles and Anglophiles sufficient for their purpose. Cecil and his mistress were not immediately interested in the secret aspirations of Lethington or of Huntly. What did concern them was to know if a Scottish statesman was prepared for the time being to support the ancient alliance or cultivate the new one. The classification rests upon that basis, and to the student of Elizabethan foreign policy its simplicity is its greatest recommendation. But it is obviously inadequate to a right understanding of the internal history of Scotland during the next ten years.

This was beyond all others the age of political inconsistency to call it by no harder name. When Machiavelli was the textbook of every European statesman, and the principles of the Company of Jesus were the general orders of the Church Militant, it is not surprising that a complete subordination of means to ends should have become habitual to most minds. There are periods of desperate conflict—and the sixteenth century was one—when men are in no position to pick and choose their weapons or their company. Self-preservation is their first instinct. We, if we would do any sort of justice to such men, must estimate them by the objects they pursued, not by the number of times they deserted a faction or betrayed a friend.

Two extreme parties, the aims and methods of which are sufficiently well-known, may be dismissed in a few words. A respectable and compact minority, but still a minority, had set before itself this task, the establishment of the Protestant religion and a permanent provision for its ministers. This was the goal they sought, looking neither to the right nor left, and regardless of every consideration of national honour or interest which came between them and the attainment of their end. They had the powerful leadership of the preachers, foremost among whom were Knox and Craig, ·while the feudal forces of Glencairn, who almost alone among his peers was a Protestant by conviction, were always at their disposal. The prosperous trading communities of Fife and the Lothians made up the rank and file of the party. To England, which was nominally Protestant, they looked for their chief support, not because they loved the English, or the English Episcopate, which they regarded as little better than the Roman "harlot," but because their terror of the Guises and the Pope drove them into the arms of Elizabeth. The continuance of her favour must be procured at any cost, by a dishonourable Union, if need be, for a dishonourable Union did not seem too high a price to pay for the security of the reformed religion.

Directly pitted against these were those furious members of the Roman Church, who, to restore the ancient faith, would have been content to see Scotland an appanage of France. They too were a minority, smaller than their opponents, and daily declining. True, they numbered several considerable families, such as the Setons, but Huntly, who of all their leaders could count on the largest following, was a man of no discretion. The most active of their company were the dispossessed priesthood, who were animated with all the bitterness natural to those that have lost both wealth and status. John Leslie, Bishop of Ross, rivalled Knox in the violence of his language and the intemperance of his bigotry.

But the game of politics in Scotland was played for other prizes than religion. Through all the intricate mazes of that game no policy is easier to trace than that of the Hamiltons. It was one of undiluted selfishness. The Duke of Chatelherault, their head, was next of kin to the reigning house. A woman, young indeed, but a widow, and still childless, was all that stood between them and the crown. Her death, or her marriage with Arran, Chatelherault's heir, would mean the realisation of their hopes. But her constitution was good, and Arran, who was half crazy, was scarcely to be suggested to so splendid a princess. There had been a time, when the precarious chances of her life as a child of eight days old, were the sole obstacle to their ambition. Clearly fortune had been against them, but the possibilities were still great, and they laboured hard to make them greater. The family were heart and soul in the work, and Chatelherault, a feeble statesman, of whom the best that can be said is the dubious praise that his intentions were excellent, was a mere tool in the hands of his more determined kinsmen.

Though such a policy could reflect but little credit on those who pursued it, there was another which disgraced the entire nation. On the eve of some momentous change it often happens that from the fermentations of a people there is bred a class of men who fatten on the public distresses. The Sixteenth Century was prolific in such, the mercenaries of the Reformation as they have been aptly termed. Scotland, where the Spartan poverty of the country has too often been associated with a Spartan avarice in her statesmen, furnished her full share. They had grown rich by the ruin of the Church, but their cupidity was greater than their need. The fear of losing what they had already won constrained them to affect the Protestant party ; the expectation of adding to it made them the docile instruments of Elizabeth, who was bound to maintain some sort of a faction in Scotland to counteract the influence of the Guises. The most notorious of this disreputable crew was James Douglas, Earl of Morton. History has dealt over kindly with him, remembering that he was a Protestant, forgetting that his greed made him so. Chastity, mercy, and patriotism, had no meaning for him; all were sacrificed to the consuming lust of gold. His fidelity to his English paymasters is the one redeeming feature of his character. To the English queen, through every change of fortune, his

". . . faith unfaithful kept him falsely true."

The separate existence of a fifth party has been as in-
adequately recognised by the contemporary historians as by
their successors. Professing in the main the reformed
opinions, and acting as a rule in unison with the followers
of Knox, the Moderates, as their attitude towards the religious question entitles us to call them, have been very
generally identified with their Extremist allies. But the
coalition was dictated rather by policy than by any real
community of aim. Knox courted the protection of England
on behalf of his reformed church. If Elizabeth's price was
the recognition of the obsolete, feudal, claim of the supremacy of the English crown, he for one was prepared to pay
it. But the fifth party sought the Union for its own sake.
Though Tudor arrogance and Scottish sensitiveness had
combined to retard it, the advantages which would accrue
from it to both countries had long been obvious to all thinking men. Only the method of agreement was in doubt. The
ideal of the Unionist party in Scotland, " the mark at which
they shot," to use the favorite phrase of Maitland of Lethington, one of the most distinguished of their number, was
the unification of the two crowns in the person of a Scottish
prince. Failing that, such a matrimonial arrangement as
was spoiled by Edward the Sixth's rough courtship, they
would not have considered derogatory to the national honour.
What they insisted on was that the Union should be treated
as a form of contract, and the consenting parties as equals.
Once it was effected, the religious question might safely be
left to work itself out as it would. In the meantime they
refused to allow the zeal of theologians to precipitate the
nation into an unpatriotic bargain.

Their position in the country it would be easy to under
estimate. The counsels of moderation are at all times
partially drowned in the united clamour of fanatical factions.
But the taunt, so commonly levelled against statesmen of this
class, that they are an army of officers alone, flies wide of the.
present mark. The names of Argyle, Athol and Mar, are
proof positive of a substantial following in the country. And
there is indirect testimony of a more convincing kind.
During the first four years of Mary's reign Scotland was
governed by her brother and her secretary, undeterred by the
armed resistance of Huntly or the impotent disgust of Knox.
Throughout that time, and probably till the day of his death,
the Lord James was the most popular man in the kingdom.
If there was one party which was actuated by unselfish love
of country, and which really merited the appellation of
" national," it was the party that was represented in the field
by Kirkcaldy of Grange, in the council-hall by Maitland of
Lethington, and in the hearts of the people by the " good
Regent."

When Mary landed at Leith in August, 1561, she found that in accepting her brother's invitation she had not been deceived. It was a strong Government that awaited her, but its strength was likely to be taxed to the uttermost. It had begun with a curt dismissal of the French ambassador, who came demanding a breach with England and a renewal of the old alliance. But, despite this testimony of good faith, relations with Elizabeth were not wholly satisfactory. Mary persistently refused to ratify the treaty of Edinburgh, and her ministers concurred in that refusal. The clause, in which she pledged herself to abstain "in all times coming" from bearing the English title, might conceivably be construed as a resignation of her claim to succeed Elizabeth, an indisputable right, which she very properly refused to sign away. The assumption of the "arms and style" of England had been at once an insult and a menace, and Elizabeth had been justly indignant; but the girl-wife was never responsible for that assumption, and she had long since abandoned it. In France she told Throckmorton that those who made the treaty made it without her authority, and the excuse served its turn. But it was obviously inconsistent with her recognition of the *status quo*. Elizabeth refused the Lord James' request that she should nominate Mary her successor, and declined to allow her cousin a safe-conduct to her own country. It was an unpleasant deadlock, and one from which there was no apparent prospect of escape.

In Scotland, the moderation of the Government, backed as it was by a certain quiet strength, disgusted and alarmed the factions. The Calvinists were the first whose disappointment got the better of all reason and good manners. The celebration of mass in Mary's private chapel was the signal for a howling mob to invade the palace. But they recoiled in astonishment from the Lord James, who kept the door with his drawn sword. "And so," says Knox, "the godly departed with great grief of heart." Another display of intolerance was more rudely checked. The Provost of Edinburgh included in his proclamation against notorious evil livers all "mass priests and obstinate papists." Mary committed him to prison, and authorised her loyal subjects to come and go as they pleased. Such backsliding was altogether lamentable, but there was worse to follow. The preachers had long enjoyed in anticipation the revenues of the disestablished church. Unfortunately the laity were in possession, and the new government showed no disposition to oust them. Beyond appropriating one third of the monies to the Crown, which had much need of it, they took but a languid interest in the dividing of the spoil.

From Lethington, the godless, scoffing, Lethington, the child of the pagan Renaissance, who had dared to sneer at the "Book of Discipline" as a "devout imagination," such indifference had been expected. But the Lord James was a serious and convinced Protestant, whose example, if only by reason of his rank and popularity, was certain to find imitators. Yet even he was fast degenerating into a mere worldling. In 1562 he married Agnes Keith, the daughter of the Earl Marischal—a happy match, and one that found favour in the Queen's eyes. Despite the admonition of Knox "to behave themselves moderately in all things," the wedding festivities were celebrated on a magnificent scale, and extended over several days, whereby "the godly" were much scandalised. Finally the Queen presented her brother with the Earldom of Mar, which, as it was found to belong of right to Erskine, was replaced by that of Moray. "The matter fell so hot betwixt the Earl of Moray and some others of the Court, and John Knox, that familiarly after that time they spoke not together more than a year and a half."

But the Calvinists, thunder as they might, could not afford to break with the Government, who after all were their best friends. For though Elizabeth was prepared for her own sake to guarantee them against extinction, she had a cordial aversion to them and their mouthpiece, the "First Blast" of whose trumpet was eternally ringing in her ears. The real danger lay in such a coalition of Hamiltons and Papists as five years earlier had confronted Mary of Guise. To both these factions Moray's influence with his sister was an object of jealous suspicion. The old slander, which clung to him through life, was revived for the occasion by the Earl of Huntly. But Mary heard it with indifference. The chronicles of the period are filled with plots and rumours of plots. Something of Huntly's ambitious projects Mary knew upon the best authority, and doubtless Moray and Lethington were sufficiently informed. A royal progress was made through the country of the Gordons, where Huntly ruled like an independent prince, and where he had the temerity to shut the gates of her own fortress of Inverness in Mary's face. In a subsequent attack upon the handful of troops that accompanied her, he paid for his indiscretion with his life.

This affair forms one of the stock charges against Moray. Yet Huntly was obviously a rebel, or at best the leader of a belligerent faction. There was nothing peculiarly atrocious in the end that overtook him. The sting of the accusation lies in the fact that Moray's new estates adjoined, if they were not actually incorporated with, the territory of the Gordons. The inference is that Moray organised the expedition, that he might utilise the forces of the Crown in expelling the present occupants. Were this established, it would not amount to much. After all, the lands belonged of right to Moray. But the device, if it was a device, was clumsily executed. More than once the Queen's liberty and her brother's life were imperilled through the weakness of their escort. Moray's detractors are at this disadvantage, that the inherent probability of any one of their conclusions is never greater than its inherent improbability. Their best endeavours go to show that, if he was a villain, he was the luckiest or the adroitest villain that ever lived.

Meanwhile the work of administration was carried on with a vigour that was new to Scottish politics. Moray, in person, undertook the dangerous task of suppressing Border lawlessness. His severity, while it made him unpopular with the professional thieves, who traded on the hostility of the two countries, was warmly approved by the Unionist party. The existence of a class, directly interested in keeping the nations asunder, was a permanent obstacle to the attainment of their ideal. But all their hopes were dashed, when after four years of strong, successful rule the Government went to pieces like a pack of cards over the question of the Queen's marriage.

When Mary made up her mind to marry Darnley, she was more irritated against Elizabeth than in love with her boyish cousin. Elizabeth had steadfastly opposed all continental alliances, not the least splendid or the least feasible of which had been the Spanish, and Mary had cheerfully acquiesced, hoping to elicit in return some pronouncement on the subject that was nearest her heart, the English succession. It makes no difference whether Leicester was seriously suggested or not. Leicester would have been welcome at Holyrood, had he brought with him an explicit recognition of Mary's title. She was pleased with Darnley, but she never felt for him that passion, which must have been latent in such a nature as hers. Realising that she had nothing to gain from the English Queen, in a fit of womanly pique she turned her back upon the policy of the last four years.

When the match was first mooted, Moray and Lethington viewed it with favour, believing it to be acceptable to both nations and to both princesses. That they subsequently changed their opinion, was due entirely to Elizabeth's affectation of displeasure. If the marriage was to destroy the good understanding that prevailed between the Governments, they were bound to oppose it. Though Darnley was of the blood royal of both nations, there was no intrinsic advantage in the alliance, which could compensate for a rupture with England. But Elizabeth never contemplated such a rupture. Indeed she had good reason to congratulate herself upon the harmlessness of Mary's choice. And Lethington was quick to suspect the outpourings of her wrath. As soon as he was convinced of their unreality, he promptly withdrew his opposition to the match.

For Lethington never lost touch with the great principle of his party. All the talk about the tortuousness of his policy is merely idle. The accomplished exponent of any game is often tempted to display more of his skill than is strictly necessary to the overthrow of his antagonist. But to say that the Secretary preferred to tread the darker paths of statecraft, is only to repeat that he was a politician of the century which produced Machiavelli and the Guises.

The less astute Moray was deceived by the imposition, or discovered it all too late. His enemies had grasped their opportunity. A combination was already on foot, which, under the pretence of furthering the match, aimed solely at the destruction of the Government. The Queen was angry and determined, and ready to welcome any who would support her against her minister. Rizzio was her confidential secretary. Morton, hoping much from Darnley's Douglas blood, and the Catholic Earls expecting everything from his religion, were zealous on his behalf. Even the infamous Bothwell, who had plotted with Huntly and the Hamiltons to assassinate the common enemy, dared to show his face at Court, but Moray was still strong enough to scare him back to his retreat. Only the Calvinists denounced the match. They professed to see in it the restoration of the ancient faith and the undoing of the Reformation. Moray took up their cry, which, though it may have been genuine in the mouth of a fanatic like Glencairn, was insincere in his. He at least must have known that no fresh danger menaced his religion, that no Popish conspiracy was in existence, beyond the permanent and unconcealed conspiracy of the Guises and their allies.

It was the greatest mistake of his life. It was indeed a triple error of judgment. He misjudged the character of Elizabeth, when he concluded, from the explosions of her wrath, that she was seriously opposed to the marriage. He misjudged the character of Darnley, when he imagined, on the strength of a few boastful utterances, that that shallow youth had either the purpose or the power to ruin him. And finally he misjudged the character of his sister, when he thought to turn her from her path by a display of armed resistance. He failed as he deserved to fail, and to the party and the nation the consequences were disastrous.

The events of the two years, which intervened between the Runabout Raid and Carberry Hill, are perhaps better known than any in Scottish history. But Moray's is no longer the most conspicuous figure. Half the time he was abroad. The stage was cleared for other actors, whose operations he is ridiculously alleged to have directed from afar. The truth is that, for the first eight months, at any rate, he was very much in the shade. On the day that his sister, riding with pistols at her saddle bow, chased him ignominiously across the Border, he awoke to the full extent of the blunder he had committed. Unlike, with one or two notable exceptions, to the great majority of his race, he possessed that invaluable quality in a statesman, patience. He could do, what Mary could never do, bide his time, and play the waiting game. Undaunted by his misfortune, he instantly set to work to retrieve it. Those, who talk of the meanness of his conduct in exile, confound diplomacy with despair. Through taking her too seriously, he had involved Elizabeth in awkward complications with the Powers. The prearranged scene, in which Moray on his knees in the presence of the ambassadors of France and Spain protested that he himself had been the sole author of the rebellion, was the penalty he paid for his mistake. In a sense it was humiliating, but that is a foolish and unprofitable pride which forbids a man to repair the consequences of his own errors.

The murder of Rizzio called Moray back to Scotland, but not to power. It was not by his party, nor in his interest, that the deed was done. The Royal Marriage had failed to gratify the anticipations of Morton. He had thought that, with his weak kinsman on the throne, the House of Douglas, of which he was the head, would govern Scotland. But he was bitterly disappointed. Mary, guided and encouraged by her Italian secretary, and daily becoming more estranged from her husband, kept a tight hand upon her prerogatives. On the advice of her uncles she called a Parliament to confiscate the estates of the exiled lords. The same Parliament, had it ever met, would have scrutinised Morton's own title to certain ecclesiastical properties. The knowledge of this precipitated Rizzio's doom, which was already determined. It was a Douglas plot, carried out by the Douglas family and their friends, and intended to make a Douglas sole King of Scotland. Of the moderate party Lethington was in the secret. Hatred of the Italian and anxiety lest Moray should be ruined secured his passive support, and he welcomed any opportunity of opening Mary's eyes to the true character of the men that were about her.

Moray knew that Rizzio was to be removed, but he knew no more, except that it was no disinterested attachment to his own person which had suggested the murder. Of the inhuman details of the plot he was never informed. He had no influence in the counsels of the conspirators, though he profited incidentally by their success. He may be censured for conniving at the assassination, but hardly for taking advantage of it.

A broad and liberal interpretation of the Sixth Commandment had ever been a national failing. Norman Leslie, the contriver of the foul murder of Cardinal Beaton, which, be it remembered, was no religious or political crime, but the outcome of a private quarrel, was regarded in his day as the flower of the Scottish youth, a judgment he confirmed by dying in the service of France like the veriest paladin. Young Kirkcaldy of Grange, his fellow conspirator, lived to acquire the reputation of a Scottish Bayard. Such facts shed a broad light upon the condition of public opinion. In a country where the men who slaughtered Beaton suffered no permanent condemnation, to have personally assisted in the removal of the upstart foreigner was something of an honour, to have acquiesced in it very far from being a reproach.

Mary and her brother met with demonstrations of joy upon her part and of sorrow upon his. He was visibly affected when she " embraced and kissed him, alleging that if he had been at home he would not have suffered her to have been so uncourteously handled." But in the midst of her distress she was still a match for her enemies. With consummate skill she won Darnley to her side, and so completely turned the tables upon Morton and his associates that they fled for safety to Newcastle, to the very quarters which the restored lords had but newly vacated. Moray regarded their discomfiture with complaisance. He owed his return to accident, not to their design, and he was too good a Stuart to view his sister's subjection to the House of Douglas with equanimity. And if he had the will, he had not the power to help them. When Mary forgave him she restored him to favour, but not to his old authority.

Bothwell was now become her chief adviser. He was a man of no principles, and of a courage and intellect not far removed from mediocrity. But boundless ambition, supported by an overbearing manner and a rashness of conduct, which were often mistaken for intrepidity, was destined to carry him far. Though nominally a Protestant, he appropriated without scruple the money which was sent from England to assist the besiegers of Leith. In those days he aimed at becoming the first minister, perhaps the husband, of Mary of Guise. At her death, the transference of his hopes to her daughter brought him into sharp conflict with Moray. Charged with compassing his rival's murder he withdrew from court, only to return when the Government was tottering. He attached himself to no party, but made it his policy to impress the Queen with a great idea of his chivalrous devotion to her service. And at last his efforts were bearing fruit. Moray, Darnley, Morton, all had failed her. She leant, in her loneliness, on the Hepburn as on one with whose loyal aid she might yet consolidate her power and inflict condign chastisement on her enemies.

The life of the miserable and deserted Darnley was now the main obstacle to the attainment of his great ambition, a marriage with the Queen. But it was an obstacle unlikely to detain him long. Casting about for a suitable confederate, he persuaded the Queen to pardon Morton, who thirsted to wreak his vengeance on the poor tool that had broken in his hands. Their machinations culminated in the blowing up of the Kirk-of-Field, an event which both Moray and his sister must have foreseen, but which the one had no power, and the other no desire, to prevent.

Bothwell was playing a winning game. There was no force at the back of popular indignation which could bring him to justice for his crime or deter him from the consummation of his hopes. Moray did not attempt to conceal his disgust, but he had learned in a bitter school the inexpediency of revolt. After flatly refusing to sign any " band " or lend any countenance to the projects of the murderer, he sought and with some little difficulty obtained leave to travel, " for he saw troubles breeding in which he loved not to have a hand."

He was in France when Mary so fatally committed herself in the eyes of Scotland and of Europe by marrying the assassin of her husband. Certainly it was wrong in her to have connived at Darnley's death, yet no one, who is acquainted with the revolting circumstances of Rizzio's murder, can doubt that it was natural. But to marry Bothwell was sheer madness. When Mary conceived that by a union with the most potent of her subjects she would strengthen her own position, she showed herself but a poor politician. She was only doing Morton's work to perfection. Morton had no further use for Bothwell, and would fain be rid of him, but his single strength was unequal to the task. Mary, by marrying him, united all parties in Scotland against him, while she injured herself irreparably in the eyes of the world.

Such was the purely political aspect of the affair, which remains undisturbed by the state of Mary's affections. She may have loved him, or she may not. He certainly cared no more for her than for a dozen other women, including his lawful wife. It would not be wonderful, if she should have felt warmly towards the one man, who had exhibited an apparently unselfish attachment to her person. But nothing can excuse the gigantic folly of her conduct. She was ruined, as the majority of princes have been ruined, by indiscretion rather than by wickedness.

The Moderate party, under the leadership of Grange, combined with Morton and his followers, and the Calvinist forces of Glencairn. The safety of the infant prince, and vengeance on the murderers of his father, were the ostensible causes of rebellion. At Carberry Hill, hard by the battlefield of Pinkie, the armies came face to face on the 15th of June, 1567.

What followed stands in no need cf re-telling. The unsteadiness of Bothwell's troops, his defiance of his enemies and precipitate flight, the courtesy of Grange, the surrender of Mary, her ungentle reception by the soldiery,—the whole scene is vivid from long familiarity. But one feature of it demands attention. It was to no peer of the realm, no Morton or Lindsay or Ruthven, that the Queen of Scots resigned the custody of her person, but to a simple laird. She knew, as she had always known, who were the true friends of her family, and in sending for Kircaldy of Grange, the first gentleman as well as the first soldier in Scotland, she was guided as much by unerring, feminine instinct, as by sad experience. Her bitter enemies have affected to see the policy of the crafty diplomat in this spontaneous action of a friendless creature. Grange's subsequent desertion of his old allies they ascribe to the gratified vanity of that hour, when the most fascinating woman in Europe placed her life in his hands. But this is mere partisanship. Grange was no " little Douglas " of Lochleven, he was no longer even young, and it was late in the day for him to succumb to the influence of the mistress he had known and served for seven years. Moreover, his genius was yet to be responsible for the victory of Langside, and the ultimate destruction of Mary's cause. Some allowance may be made for the temper of men, conscious that nothing but their own violence has alienated the sympathy of the noblest among their countrymen. But later critics have no excuse for shutting their eyes to facts, or for persistently confounding the greedy instruments of Cecil with the patriots, who were only constrained by the unhappy condition of their country to keep such disreputable company.

When the news of Carberry Hill and Lochleven reached Paris, Moray perceiving that it was time for him to act, and meeting with no opposition from the authorities, set out for the coast. Forewarned that the Archbishop of Glasgow, Mary's resident at the French Court, was endeavouring to procure his detention, he made all speed to Dieppe, crossed the Channel unmolested, and passing quietly through England, was met at Berwick by Sir James Melville, who had been deputed by the Moderate party to discuss the situation with their old leader.

By the advice of Lethington and Athol, Mary had abdicated in favour of her son. No menaces of Elizabeth's, no blusterings of the French Court, could alter the fact that James the Sixth was the anointed king of Scotland, and that, as far as Morton was concerned, he was likely to remain so. But the Moderate party never intended that the arrangement should be permanent. It was merely a makeshift which must stand till Bothwell was destroyed, and the memory of the Queen's indiscretion had faded from the public mind. If Moray accepted the Regency to carry on the policy his party had already initiated, Mary would yet be reinstated. But should he hold aloof, or should there be the slightest misunderstanding or divergence of opinion, the plan would, in all probability, prove abortive. To cope successfully with Morton and his following, they must have a unanimous party in complete accord with its leader.

This was the second time that Moray had returned to Scotland to find his sister in the hands of that disloyal Douglas, whose very name was of evil omen to the House of Stuart. He saw at a glance that her life was in actual danger, as much from her false friends as from her avowed enemies. It was darkly rumoured that the Hamiltons had asked for her assassination as the price of their support. It was certain that if they attempted to raise the country in her favour, Morton would kill her without scruple, and that the Calvinists, with Knox at their head, would applaud the murder, as the act of God. Whether her ultimate restoration were feasible or not, Moray was bound by every obligation, public and private, to insure her immediate safety. He would be doing the worst disservice in the world, both to her and to Scotland, if he allowed the Regency to devolve on a committee of nobles, whose nerveless counsels would be dominated from the outset by the vigorous genius of Morton.

In such considerations Moray's slanderers may seek their answer. It was mere weakness of political insight, which made certain of his friends find fault with his behaviour on the occasion of the famous interview at Lochleven. They did not know, or they did not allow for the fact, that Mary was perhaps the one person in Scotland most ignorant of the perils that environed her, that, though Lindsay's brutality might terrify her for the time, it could not awaken her to a real consciousness of her danger. They never weighed the difficulty of convincing such a woman that her strength was to sit still, that the quiet policy of her friends would in due course bring about that restoration to popularity and power, which any intrigue with the Hamiltons, the enemies of her claims, and any premature attempts to escape from her prison, would assuredly lose her for ever. And yet on the condition of Mary's mind, the whole success of their policy depended. Better than Melville, better than Throckmorton, Moray grasped the situation, and took instinctively the proper course. Perhaps, he thought, if the brother she had loved and honored, and whose return from exile and disgrace she had welcomed, when first she knew her dead husband for what he was, perhaps if he came and acted the "ghostly father" to her, as Throckmorton has it, at last she might

understand. If he could not scare her into common sense,
no living man could. It must have cost him something to
speak to his sister as, by his own admission, he spoke to her.
But it was the kindest cruelty he ever showed her, and it met
with a fair measure of success. If he did not secure her
acquiescence in his policy, he convinced her of her immediate
jeopardy.

This is not the place to attempt to penetrate the historic
mystery of the Casket Letters. Their mere existence, quite
apart from the question of their authenticity, was the ugliest
factor in the problem which the Regent had to face. Either
they were genuine, or they were not. In the former case he
could not refuse to recognise them, still less could he hope to
destroy them. Morton would take care of that. They were
Morton's property, they had been in his possession for three
weeks, they could be relied on to furnish a triumphant vindi-
cation of his recent conduct. If, on the other hand, they
were spurious, or some, or all of them had been tampered
with, either the Regent was deceived, as even Norfolk was
afterwards deceived, or he knew them to be fabricated, and
could form a shrewd guess as to the manner and purpose
of their fabrication. But even supposing him to have known
or conjectured so much, how was it possible for him to expose a fraud, which Mary herself, when the time came, could
not expose ? If the Casket Letters were forgeries, they were
the cleverest in all history. In either case, the Regent, who
had been hard put to it to save his sister's life, was in no
plight to treat them cavalierly. True or false, Morton had
got them, and would not hesitate to use them. To him and
to Cecil they were invaluable. Round them was to be fought
out the closest diplomatic struggle of the next eighteen
months.

It was now that the Regent made the second mistake of
his political career. The Hamiltons, and those of the aris-
tocracy, who, like Argyle, still held aloof from the new
Government, becoming conscious of their own weakness,
sent to request a conference with the King's party. On the
frivolous pretext that they had neglected to style the Regent
by his proper title, no answer was vouchsafed, an error of
judgment, which was paid for dearly enough. This was the
work of Morton and his confederates, who formed a clear
majority on the Council, and whose obvious policy was to
drive the House of Hamilton into desperate courses, that
they might share the spoils of its downfall among themselves.

It was no brilliant opportunity of uniting a divided nation,
which the Regent had lost. The Hamiltons were never to
be trusted, at the best they would have been but dangerous
allies. Still, there were men among them, Argyle and

Herries for example, who were worth conciliating, and the King's Government was sufficiently strong to make advances without fear of their being misunderstood. Moreover it was necessary to the success of that policy, which Melville had unfolded at Berwick, that Hamilton should not be allowed to become a focus of disaffection, whereof they might expect an abundant increase, as soon as the Regent got to work on the Borders and elsewhere. Mary's name would be made a rallying cry, and Mary herself, plunging madly into some fantastic scheme for her forcible restoration, would ruin her cause for ever.

In May 1568 all Scotland was electrified by the news of the Queen's escape from Lochleven. At Hamilton six thousand men were gathering about her. The Regent, who had been holding a justice court at Glasgow, only ten miles away, was totally unprepared to take the field. For the first time he saw the full magnitude of his mistake, and made haste to atone for it. It was one of those occasions, which test the real greatness of a man, and never was he seen to more advantage. Realising that the immediate danger was preferable to a demoralising retreat, he stood his ground, though many counselled otherwise. In obedience to his summons, the territorial magnates of the King's party called out their feudal arrays. So rapidly did his strength increase, that he was enabled to march from Glasgow with an army of over four thousand men, to intercept the Queen's forces, which were moving on Dumbarton. He was too good a general not to estimate his own talents at their proper worth. While retaining the nominal command for himself, he gave Grange a free hand, with disastrous results to his enemies. That veteran made short work of their raw valour. It was an easy victory, and only his and Grange's natural humanity saved it from becoming a massacre.

It is melancholy reading how on the very morning of the battle there had still been hopes of reconciliation. Mary had requested Melville to procure the co-operation of Lethington and Grange in promoting an amicable settlement. But it was too late. The Hamiltons, confident in their numbers and their courage, were already pushing on to carry the village of Langside. They only precipitated the catastrophe. Within three days Mary Stuart was in Cumberland.

She had chosen the lesser of two evils. Elizabeth, it is true, was an enemy, but an enemy rather to her claims than to her personality. Moreover, she was known to hold high views on the divinity of kings. Certainly England was to be preferred to France and the she-devil who was all powerful there.

Materially as Elizabeth's hands were strengthened by the possession of Mary's person, her situation for the time being became one of extreme delicacy. There was plenty to dissatisfy and alarm her in recent events. It had been one thing to embarrass a strong Government by tampering with its disaffected subjects, it was another, and a totally different thing, when a Queen and a kinswoman came flying for her life from the insurrectionary forces of her own countrymen. Elizabeth felt the full danger of this precedent of armed resistance to divine authority, and she felt it all the more keenly now that it had proved successful. What if the principle were more extensively applied, so as to include within its scope the fabric of Tudor absolutism? The bare contingency was of itself sufficient to make her walk most warily in her dealings with the victorious party. Then again there was Mary demanding, with considerable appearance of reason and justice, to be forcibly reinstated. Mary had friends in Scotland and more dangerous friends in England, but for the present both she and they must be disregarded. Cecil could be relied on to keep them amused, while the English Government turned to meet the more pressing peril of foreign intervention. They could trifle with the Romish party on both sides of the border, but they could not trifle with the representatives of France and Spain, who were instructed to insist in unmistakable terms on an explanation of the detention of the Queen of Scots and of the complacency shown to her rebellious subjects.

The difficulty was no ordinary one, but they were no ordinary statesmen that were confronted with it. To satisfy the courts of Paris and Madrid, to retain possession of Mary's person, and at the same time to do the least possible injury to the common cause of monarchy, that was the threefold problem presented for the solution of Elizabeth and her advisers. They went to work with the rare political sagacity characteristic of the times. The famous Commission of York, a tribunal unique in the history of judicature, was Elizabeth's answer at once to the princes of the continent, to the Queen of Scots, and to her own conscience. The whole unfortunate business should be thoroughly and impartially sifted, but royalty should come by no detriment in the process. Through the voice of its representatives the rebellious Scottish nation should be heard on its defence before the Commissioners of the English Crown. Such was the equitable language which Elizabeth held to Mary and the ambassadors, but such was very far from being her secret aim. To compel Moray for his own safety to accuse his sister of her husband's murder, and to extort from him a written copy of the accusation, was the intention of the English Government in appointing the Commission. So would Mary's reputation be blasted and the voice of Europe silenced for ever.

In Scotland the Estates had met, and the influence of Lethington and the Regent's own inclination had combined to procure the adoption of a lenient policy towards the defeated faction. The Knoxians chafed, but the Moderate party were still uppermost although their time was short. Opposition smouldered in the country, and the Regent, taking the field a second time, carried everything before him. But he was stayed in his victorious progress by indignant letters from Elizabeth, wherein she demanded an explanation of his attitude towards his Sovereign and desired him to appoint representatives to the Commission at York.

There can be little doubt that, irritated by the peremptory tone of this missive, the Regent's first impulse was to repudiate the indignity of pleading before foreign judges. The Moderate party, as a whole, were dead against any such course. Not only did they consider it an infamy to submit their cause to the judgment of English subjects, but they feared for the consequences to the safety and the honour of their Queen. Before this Commission, with its vague and ill-defined powers, there was no knowing what influences might be exerted, what intrigues set on foot. Lethington, who, it may be confidently averred, had fathomed the schemes of Cecil from the first, recommended the Regent to refuse point blank to have a hand in such proceedings.

But there was another and a wider aspect of the matter which could not be lost sight of. The Regent's enemies in Scotland were numerous, and, though crushed for the moment, would assuredly give trouble. Abroad, France under the Guises was his implacable foe. Could he, at the present juncture, afford to lose the friendship of Elizabeth, was the question which, upon reflection, presented itself with increasing force. Lethington might argue that there was no good ground for anxiety, that he was as necessary to Elizabeth as Elizabeth was to him, that under no circumstance would she, or could she, tolerate the presence of French troops on Scottish soil. But such reasoning hardly carried conviction. If Mary came with an English army at her back, no power on earth could save them or their cause from total ruin. The Union would indeed be effected, but after a very different fashion from "the mark at which Lethington shot." The theory of English jurists would become a melancholy fact, and a vassal Queen of Scots would yield allegiance to her English suzerain.

Whether Morton and his circle understood precisely what was required of them by their paymasters, makes no material difference. Whatever it was they were prepared to do it. Three out of the five Commissioners appointed in the name of " James, by the grace of God, King of Scots," were Morton, Lindsay, and their creature, the Bishop of Orkney, who was anxious to compensate by present zeal for the invidious part he had so recently played in the marriage ceremony with Bothwell. The learned Buchanan, too, was at their service, and such inferior mercenaries as MacGill and Wood. The Regent nominated himself upon the Commission, because, it is said, none other of suitable rank would accept the post. That he should, on so trivial a ground, have incurred the peril of leaving his work half finished, is of itself incredible. It was Scotland's honour and his sister's, neither of which was safe in Morton's keeping, that summoned him to York. They summoned Lethington also, who accompanied the Commissioners, not, as the story goes, by compulsion of the Regent, who was afraid to leave him behind, but of his own deliberate choice, and for the better protection of his country and his beloved mistress. With him went Sir James Melville, Henry Balnaves, and others of the Moderate party, all as determined as himself to preserve their leader from the machinations of Morton and of Cecil.

But before the Commission met, the Regent made a desperate effort to escape the toils that were fast closing about him. He forwarded copies of the Casket Letters to England with a request to know what action would be taken, supposing he should prove his case. Experience had taught him that to pursue such a course with the English Queen was nothing more than ordinary caution. But it must have taught him also that any assurances he might receive would be of little value. His real designs went deeper. He was playing off Elizabeth's theory of divine right against her desire to ruin her rival. He was trying to frighten her into the belief that he possessed such damning evidence of his sister's guilt, that its mere production would compel her to bring Mary to a trial. To escape such a contingency she might even recall the warrant for the Commission, at any rate she would be deterred from pushing him to extremities, when he did appear at York. It was a bold move, and a skilful, not unworthy of himself and Lethington, but it failed, if for no other reason, because Cecil, divining its intention, kept back the copies from the Queen.

Early in October, 1568, the extraordinary conference began its sittings in the historic northern capital. Mary's representatives were seven in number, the Protestant Lord Herries and the devoted Bishop of Ross being the most distinguished. The Duke of Norfolk, the Earl of Essex, and Sir Ralph Sadler appeared on behalf of Elizabeth. From the very outset the enquiry was a farce, as indeed it was bound to be, when none of the three consenting parties consented of their own free choice. The exigencies of foreign politics had compelled Elizabeth to command it, his own dependence on her friendship had forced the Regent to participate in it, and only her utter helplessness had driven Mary to acknowledge it. The first discussion was stamped with unreality. It was protested that the Queen of Scots was really and truly above all earthly courts. To this illogicality was opposed the outworn fiction of English feudal supremacy, an acknowledgment of which was demanded from the Commissioners of the infant king. The Regent, at a loss for a reply ,turned red with shame and anger, but Lethington struck boldly in with proud, mocking words. When, he said, the two northern shires of England and the town of Berwick were restored to their rightful owner, it would be time enough to render homage where homage was due, " but as for the Crown and Kingdom of Scotland, it was freer than England had been of late, when it paid St. Peter's penny to the Pope." After this preliminary passage of wits, Mary's Commissioners formulated their charges of rebellion. Before replying, the Regent reiterated his request for a definite statement of the powers of the Commission. No satisfactory answer was forthcoming, and Lethington in disgust gave public expression to his conviction that nothing less was intended than the dishonour of their king's mother. The Regent's apology was based on general grounds and couched in temperate language, and as soon as the rebutting arguments had been heard, the English triumvirs gave out that they were dissatisfied with the case for the defence.

Inch by inch the Regent was being forced towards the inevitable precipice. So far as events had gone it is not easy to see what else he could have expected, short of the conference being broken off. But he was perfectly alive to the situation. Day and night he schemed and plotted with the tireless Lethington to save his country and his sister. Far more important than the formal proceedings of the Commission were the unofficial intrigues of the Commissioners. Of two of these some account remains, though the details of both are enveloped in a becoming atmosphere of mystery.

The Englishmen were privately shown the originals of the Casket Letters. This step, as far as the Regent and Lethington were concerned, was the natural sequel of their first attempt to work on Elizabeth's susceptibilities. A description of the contents of the casket, and of the effect produced on the minds of those that saw them, was forwarded to the English court. But nothing came of it. All that the Regent got for his pains was a specious declaration of good faith, which was neutralised by its preamble.

The other intrigue went deeper. The parties to it were Lethington and the Regent on the one hand, and the Duke of Norfolk on the other. The Duke, who was the most powerful subject in Europe and the most popular man in England, had resolved to marry Mary. At York he unfolded his project to the two leaders of the Moderate party in Scotland, and from them received direct encouragement. So much is certain. Some have regarded, or pretended to regard, the Regent's attitude as inexplicable. And inexplicable no doubt it is to those who can see in him nothing but the unnatural contriver of his sister's ruin. To others, who know him for what he really was, the most influential of her secret friends, the explanation is sufficiently simple. Norfolk and he had now one common object, the preservation of Mary's fair fame. An alliance between the leaders of two out of the three sets of Commissioners must necessarily have carried with it no little weight. Norfolk confirmed the Regent in his policy of demanding Elizabeth's sign-manual to convict, alleging that to his certain knowledge no sentence ever was, or ever would be, intended. Considerable delay ensued while posts went to and fro between London and York. Elizabeth requested the Regent to send her some one for her better information. Lethington was chosen, but Morton, who suspected his talents and his patriotism and publicly blamed him for the delay, procured him the unwelcome company of MacGill. Cecil had already begun to fear for the miscarriage of his scheme. What he learned from MacGill moved him to prevail upon the Queen to summon all to London.

The conference was resumed at Hampton Court, in the presence of the English Council. So far the Regent had played his cards well, and there was good hope that he might yet win all. But circumstances began to combine against him. In Scotland the Hamiltons, assisted by Mary's misguided friends, were busy as ever in their own interest. The country was flooded from end to end with all manner of ridiculous rumours. The Regent had been committed to the Tower, he had surrendered the custody of the infant king, he was bargaining to deliver up the fortresses. It is asserted that Sir James Balfour, a particularly active agent in the dissemination of such dangerous rubbish, took his orders from Lethington. Why Lethington should wish to force the Regent to return, so that Morton and such might be left behind unfettered, is not easy to see. But it has become a sort of habit to associate his name with the insoluble. Whoever was responsible, the circulation of these nonsensical figments produced a general feeling of unrest, which a knowledge of one at least of the tainted quarters from whence they emanated was insufficient to allay. At any other time their best refutation would have been their own folly. At the present juncture, happen what might in London, the Regent's return to his uneasy charge could not be much longer deferred.

But what was worse even than this, the Norfolk hope failed him. Something of the private proceedings at York had been very early divulged. Mary had heard, almost as soon as it was possible to hear, of the business of the Casket Letters, and had instructed her Commissioners accordingly. And now Morton had got wind of the transaction with Norfolk, and what Morton knew Cecil knew also, if he had not already unearthed it for himself. At any rate the Duke was a suspected man, and was soon to be a ruined one. He was no more in a position to make the Regent's peace with Elizabeth than he was to save Mary's honour, or, as the event proved, his own life.

On the twenty-sixth of November the end came. That day saw Mary Stuart proclaimed to the whole world "counsel, device, persuader, and commander" of the murder of her own husband. It saw also the disintegration of the party, which, with few interruptions, had governed Scotland for eight troublous years. Henceforward the figure of the captive and dishonoured Queen was to come between old friends and colleagues, separating them till death.

There is something incredible in the details of the last scene, as recorded by Melville. No doubt it is true that Elizabeth had given her verbal assurance to follow up the accusation, that the Regent, despite the opposition of the great bulk of his company, still pressed for "writ and seal," and that English and Scotch alike reproached him in no measured terms for mistrusting the word of a Queen. But when we are asked to believe that Mr. John Wood produced the document, that Orkney snatched it from his hand, and, though hotly pursued by his hypocritical accomplice, succeeded in delivering it to Cecil amid the unseemly jests and boisterous laughter of both gangs of lordly conspirators, we are moved to suspect poor Melville of romancing, to cover what seemed to him his leader's perfidy. For the credit of the two nations it is to be hoped that such were not the circumstances, which attended the publication of Mary's shame. The tale is utterly at variance with every preconceived notion of the decorous, Elizabethan court. It rather recalls, in its vulgarity, that later day, when Ireton and Harrison in bed together signed away the life of Mary's grandson. True or false—and it has all the air of having been invented by a loyal, but short-sighted, apologist—as a defence of the Regent's conduct it is mere childishness. If he had not made up his mind to present the accusation, he would never for one moment have allowed the fatal paper to pass out of his own hands. His enemies have been so weak as to accuse him of organising the stupid spectacle. But fortunately his reputation does not stand or fall by the genuineness of Melville's fantastic story. He has little enough to gain from such ingenious advocacy.

He had come at last to the parting of the ways, to one of

those supreme decisions, which mercifully fall to the lot of few. Once and for all he must choose, and choose without hope of recantation, between his sister's honour and his country's good, between the ties of blood and the settled policy of a lifetime. The dual position was no longer tenable. Something must be relinquished, if something was to be saved. He was not swept off his feet by the pressure of the mercenary crowd, which served him while they feared and envied him, nor overborne by any sudden impulse of events, least of all was he bribed into pusillanimity. Only when every resource of an accomplished statecraft had been tried in vain, when every ally had failed him and every hope was extinguished, calmly and deliberately, as a patriot and a leader, as a Scotchman and a Unionist, he made his choice.

It is said that he was arraigned at the bar of European opinion. If this imply no more than the general truth that few men tamely submit to see their motives misinterpreted, it is a platitude. If it mean that from the days of Lochleven and Langside the Regent had gone in terror of the princes of the continent, it is false. He could snap his fingers at the princes of the continent, as long as Elizabeth's friendship was assured. And the accusation of Mary was the price she asked.

But Lethington could not desert his beloved mistress. His policy and the Regent's were still substantially the same, the Union of the Crowns in the person of a Scottish prince. But which prince? To her brother it seemed that, accusation or no accusation, Mary was impossible. But her old secretary was ready and willing to take her as she was, to commit her to the generosity of her countrymen, and to begin afresh, as though the red nightmare of Rizzio and Bothwell had never come between her and the happier past. It was loyalty, chivalry, devotion, but not statesmanship. Scotland could not stand alone. To lose England was to lose all. Lethington knew, none better, that however much he might use the Guises to lower Elizabeth's tone, the policy of a French alliance belonged to an age that was already half-forgotten. The measure of the bitterness of religious hate was the measure of its impossibility. But, such is the strange irony of life, the biggest brain in Scotland was fast drifting towards the factions of unreason.

Few guessed, and few have cared to think, how much the sacrifice of his sister cost the Regent as a man, how far the great betrayal, as it was thought, was in point of fact a great renunciation. The decision to accuse meant more than the abandonment of Mary; it meant the destruction of the national party and the loss of lifelong friends. Only those—and happily they are not many—who have been confronted with some such momentous issue, can ever conceive of the intensity of his agony. Externally impassive as he was by nature and training, he broke down at the last, and, in the words of one who saw him, "went forth of the council-house with tears in his eyes."

Little of interest occurred before the conference died out of its own inanition. Mary's Commissioners were instructed, in defiance of their own better judgment, to bring a counter-accusation of complicity in Darnley's murder against the Regent and his colleagues. It was met, of course, with a fierce denial, and, being unsupported by evidence of any sort, did more harm to Mary than to her adversaries. After a little swagger between Herries and Lindsay, the professional bully of Morton's set, the matter was allowed to drop. Finally, the feeble Chatelherault was goaded by his friends into claiming the Regency as his natural right, but he met with a chilly reception from Elizabeth, whose mind was now made up. She had conquered her monarchical scruples, and was bent on supporting the title of the infant king. As for the accusation and the documentary evidence which accompanied it, she was as little desirous of pushing it as the Regent, and Mary would not condescend to reply to it. It remained an indelible stigma on the reputation of the Scottish Queen, a respectable argument for her detention in England, and a sufficient answer to the Powers.

The Regent was now at liberty to return. But if Elizabeth was satisfied, certain of her subjects were not. There was reason to fear that in the northern counties, where disaffection to the Protestant Government was rampant, his life would be attempted. But Norfolk's word was above the law in those parts, and Norfolk hoped to make further use of him. A hint from head quarters was sufficient to disarm the leading malcontents. In January, 1569, escorted by such a force as more than secured him against any unauthorised designs that may have been contemplated, the Regent came safely to Berwick.

All opposition to his authority at once collapsed. Not a shot was fired, not a blow struck. The surrender of the Hamiltons became a question only of weeks. In return for a general amnesty and revocation of their forfeitures, they consented to recognise the title of the infant king, to obey the Regent, and to find hostages for their loyal observance of the bargain. As these were not forthcoming, Chatelherault and Herries, the ambassadors of their party, were summarily committed to the Castle of Edinburgh, a high-handed act, that can only be justified by the suspicion in which the Hamiltons were held, and by a fresh outbreak of the Gordons in the North. With a great army at his back the Regent passed through the disaffected regions. Justice courts were held at Aberdeen, Elgin, and Inverness. By fines and confiscations the enemies of the Government were effectually crippled.

The Regent had less than twelve months of life before him, but they were busy months and sad. The border thieves renewed their old disorders, only to be crushed with signal severity. Pestilence and famine, which even at this period the best of governments were powerless to allay, made havoc of the people. But sadder for Scotland than pestilence and famine and border ruffianry was the gradual breaking up of the Moderate party. It has been seen that the appointment of Commissioners to the conference at York had been the cause of no little heart searching among the most attached followers of the Regent. On such ears the news from Hampton Court had fallen with stunning force. Men began to review their past policy, to question whether the peace, which was won at the cost of Mary's humiliation, was the peace of the Unionist ideal. Admitting that the accusation had been inevitable, was it honourable, was it even expedient, that the mother of their King should be detained in foreign prisons? If she must be confined, let her at least be confined on Scottish soil. Lochleven, it was true, had failed to hold her, but there were other fortresses besides Lochleven, and it would be strange indeed if one could not be found to keep her as securely as an English manor house. Such arguments, appealing strongly to the national reason and still more strongly to the national pride, were dangerous in any hands. In those of men formidable as Lethington and Grange were formidable, no less for their own talents than for their great and deserved popularity in the country, neither Morton nor the Regent could ignore them. Each made answer after his kind. The Regent, indeed, acting on the dictates of his own conscience, had early embarked in desperate negotiations for the recovery of his sister's person. Morton struck at the head. All his energies were directed to bringing Lethington to the scaffold.

His personal desires coincided with the orders of his paymasters. The fall of Norfolk had revealed the fact that Lethington was deeply implicated in the matrimonial plot. The rebellion of the Northern Earls was believed to be the outcome of a conspiracy, which had its ramifications in Scotland as well as England, and which aimed at the union of the two nations under Mary Stuart, the famous pet project of Lethington's life. Fear and resentment roused Elizabeth against him. The Regent was his friend, but the Regent had no longer a free hand. He took refuge with the Earl of Athol at Dunkeld, whence he maintained an epistolary correspondence with his old leader. But Mary had secret dealings with him through the agency of Seton. The breach, though not yet complete, was widening day by day.

Morton had another to reckon with besides Lethington. Grange held the Castle of Edinburgh for the young King, but Grange for once was uneasy in his conscience and uncertain of his duty. He viewed the treatment of Mary with disgust, and Morton's growing preponderance in the counsels of the Regent with the darkest suspicion. The parasites, who clustered around both, the Woods and Orkneys and McGills, were peculiarly obnoxious to him, and he to them. They knew his nobility of character, and they dreaded his talents for action no less than Lethington's for diplomacy. Like his father, the Lord High Treasurer, who was ever ready to make good his utterances with his sword, he denounced to their faces these traffickers in their country's honour. His attitude at this time is admirably illustrated by a passage in Melville. Grange, having expressed his strong disapprobation at the arrest of Herries and Chatelherault, was taken to task by Mr. John Wood: " I marvel at you," said Wood, "that you should be offended at this. For how shall we, who are my Lord's dependers, get rewards but by the wreck of such men? Yea, said Grange, is that your holiness? I see nothing among you but envy, greediness, and ambition, whereby you will wreck a good Regent and ruin the country." This was that same Wood who was offended at Henry Balnaves, "being indeed such a man as Mr. John would have appeared to be," because Balnaves flatly refused to exert his influence with the Regent to procure him the bishopric of Moray.

Grange would have preferred to withdraw from public life, but rather than desert a friend he decided to remain and, as the event proved, to sacrifice himself. Lethington had been enticed to Stirling, where Crawford of Jordanhill was put up to accuse him, on behalf of Lennox, as an aider and abettor of the late King's murder. Both he and Balfour were arrested. The latter wrote to Grange, demanding that protection which was promised him when he resigned his command of the Castle. Grange, feeling that his honour was concerned in the saving of them both, requested their release. The Regent replied that the combination on the Council was too strong for him. Grange and Herries retorted by proclaiming Douglas and Morton "airt and pairt of the King's murther," and offering, in their respective persons, to attest the same in single combat.

The challenge was unaccepted, but, as the time of trial approached, the friends and supporters of Lethington prepared to keep it in such numbers that his acquittal was felt to be a foregone conclusion. The Regent put a stop to the proceedings and committed his prisoner to the Castle, no bad testimony to his own good faith. Melville says that at this time some of Morton's assassins had instructions to deal with

Grange at the first opportunity. One cannot but think that the Earl must have known his man better. Through some misunderstanding, begotten of mutual suspicion, Lethington was detained in the city. Grange came down with a detachment of the garrison at his back, demanded the prisoner of his guards, who dared not refuse, and lodged him safely in the Castle.

The Regent's position was an unhappy one, and in a subsequent interview with Grange he failed to mend it. Far from allaying suspicion, his exaggerated protestations of friendship produced a most unfavourable impression on the mind of his old colleague. " He gave him more fair words than he was wont to do, which Grange took in evil part," wrongly, it is true, but not unnaturally. To the plain soldier it seemed that this was not emotion but effusiveness, that this man whose language was at all times singularly self-contained was playing an unaccustomed part and over-doing it. Henceforth all confidence between them was at an end.

Everywhere the Regent was losing ground. When the English rebellion broke out, he had marched an army to the border, that he might watch events, while at the same time he was in a situation to act upon them. The fugitive Northumberland fell into his hands, and was sent a prisoner to Lochleven. At once the national pride was all aflame. For what good purpose, it was asked, had that immemorial right of asylum, of which every Scot was so justly proud, been denied to this noble refugee from the vengeance of the English Government. Unfortunately there were plenty to supply an answer. Because the Regent was grasping at the crown, because he was the docile instrument of Elizabeth, because he had sold his sister to Cecil, and was about to sell him his country, because of anything but the real reason, he had done this thing. Many examples prove that there are few principles a people esteems more highly than that of an almost sacred immunity for alien offenders, more especially political offenders, and few mistakes in government they resent more bitterly than any infringement of it. Doubtless the Regent had counted the cost. He knew the temper of his proud, touchy countrymen, and was prepared to face the storm. In Northumberland he possessed a piece, which should prove of inestimable value in the game he was playing for the recovery of his sister. It was the last of many sacrifices he had made for her, and it was a heavy one, heavier perhaps than he had foreseen. The country at large knew nothing of the secret workings of his diplomacy. It could only judge by results, and it was exposed to fomented agitation. The Regent's popularity was shaken, and his enemies gave him no time to recover it.

The Hamiltons were resolved to be rid of this man, who had thwarted all their schemes and extinguished all their hopes. Once the design was formed, its execution was simple. They had only to fall back upon the habit of the age and the unvarying tradition of the country. The marvel is that living when he did, and where he did, the Regent should have escaped so long. The congenial task was allotted to one of their own name. Nowadays it would be stale to recite the fable of "injured Bothwellhaugh." and superfluous to expose it. In common with the rest of his house James Hamilton had carried arms at Langside, and suffered the customary penalties of defeat, which do not appear in his case to have been abnormally severe. There were scores of gentlemen in the same, if not in a worse plight. But his was one of those brooding natures which the contemplation of their own misfortunes drives to the verge of insanity. A knowledge of this and of his reckless hardihood guided his sagacious kinsmen in their choice.

Among the many wild scenes of Scottish history the murder of the Regent Moray stands out with melancholy prominence. Literary and pictorial art have striven to intensify a spectacle, that has little need of either,—the narrow High Street of Linlithgow, the gay procession with difficulty forcing a passage through the dense crowd which thronged about "the good Regent," the anxious faces of his friends, his own calm self-forgetfulness, and then the flash, the echoing report, the frantic rush at the barricaded door, and Bothwellhaugh galloping madly across the open country with all the proud sense of a good deed well done. Moray lingered for several hours conscious, and in great pain. It is recorded how, when some of those, that stood beside his bed, upbraided the clemency, which eighteen months before had spared the assassin, he said with characteristic gentleness, "that they should never make him forethink any good he had ever done in his life," a notable and touching speech in the mouth of one, who had a larger claim than any living man to Scotland's gratitude.

To vindicate him against Mary's literary partisans would be a hopeless task. Tried by a standard of conduct that was never his own the best of men comes badly off. The chivalry which consists in an absolute surrender to the physical fascination of a woman, the loyalty which yields unquestioning obedience to the sacrosanct personality of an anointed king, these romantic virtues, strangely destined as they were to an imperishable association with his ill-starred house, found no place in the character of Moray. But to denounce him as an unnatural brother argues a singularly shallow comprehension of the circumstances of the time. His capacity, though equal to his rank, would not by itself have been suf-

ficient to exalt him above his peers. It was just because he
was her father's son that he was strong enough to be Mary's
minister in prosperity, and partially, at any rate, her protector
in misfortune. But for him, it is urged, there would have
been no tragedy of Fotheringay. And there is a measure of
truth in the reproach. But for him, indeed, the tragedy of
Fotheringay would have been anticipated in Lochleven, or
Tantallon, or elsewhere, by twenty years.

Even the most ardent Jacobite must admit that he did his
family good service when he crushed the House of Hamilton.
At any time in his life the sceptre might, and more than once
it seemed as though it must, have passed to Chatelherault.
But the Archbishop and his kin were outwitted, and they
knew it. In so far as he fell a victim to their exasperation
he was the proto-martyr of the House of Stuart.

His difference with the party that followed him has already
been explained. Our judgment upon it must, in the long
run, depend upon ourselves. A man may feel that Lethington's choice would have been his own, and yet remain un-
convinced of the wisdom of that choice. This much is
certain. When Moray returned from Hampton Court, if
honour were indeed lost, as Grange and Lethington held, all
else was won. "The mark" at which these three had once
combined to shoot was yet to be attained in the person of
Mary's child. If success is the best justification for any
policy, Moray's was justified in 1603.

For the rest, he was a notable figure in the Europe of his
day. Strong and not cruel, reverend and not sanctimonious,
a soldier, and not a bravo, a reformer and not covetous, a
Protestant and not a traitor,—this, in the Sixteenth Century,
was a rare combination. The sincerity of his religious con-
victions and the purity of his private life have never been
challenged. He had a genuine admiration for that new
learning, which his brief, busy career left him no time to
cultivate. At his table the scholar and the theologian were
certain of a hospitable welcome. Of a naturally gentle
disposition, in an age disgraced beyond all others by civil
and religious inhumanity, and in a country where more
odium attached to moral lapses than to the shedding of
blood, he preserved a reputation for consistent clemency.
He was greater than many statesmen of his time, and he
possessed, in a greater degree than most, a moral consciousness.

And this raises a final, and perhaps a novel, question.
Did Moray wish for the end? It is said that, though he
was forewarned of Bothwellhaugh's preparations, he refused
to institute a search. It is certain that he knew his peril,
and yet neglected the most ordinary measures of precaution.
He was never the man to risk his life without a cause, much

less to fling it away in mere bravado. It may well be that he courted death, not because he was weary of living, but because he shrank from the future. Sooner or later he would be forced to deal with the occupants of the Castle, the struggle would be protracted and severe, in the event, the extreme penalty would be demanded and, with or without his consent, exacted. It may well be that he had some prescience of the day, when to sustain the mantic reputation of Knox, the foremost soldier of the Scottish Reformation would be hanged in the Grassmarket, and the brilliant Lethington driven "to end his life after the old Roman fashion." Already he had sacrificed a sister's love and an ancient friendship on the altar of his country. Who shall say that he was wholly satisfied in his own conscience of having done the right? At any rate, if he had steeled his heart against the loss of friends, he had not steeled it for their destruction. Two waves he had breasted, but he could not face the third. Suicide is ever a form of cowardice, yet that is a noble cowardice which prompts a man to lay down his life for a friend. If there be any truth in this surmise, what was said of Moray's voluntary exile after the murder of Darnley acquires a deeper and sadder meaning when applied to his own assassination. · He was seeking death when it found him, "for he saw troubles breeding, in which he loved not to have a hand."